The Leaves in October

The Leaves in October

KAREN ACKERMAN

Atheneum   New York
Collier Macmillan Canada
Toronto
Maxwell Macmillan International Publishing Group
New York   Oxford   Singapore   Sydney

Atheneum
Macmillan Publishing Company
866 Third Avenue
New York, NY 10022

Collier Macmillan Canada, Inc.
1200 Eglinton Avenue East
Suite 200
Don Mills, Ontario M3C 3N1

Printed in the United States of America
Designed by Nancy B. Williams
2   3   4   5   6   7   8   9   10

Library of Congress Cataloging-in-Publication Data
Ackerman, Karen, 1951–
The leaves in October/by Karen Ackerman.—1st ed.
p.   cm.
Summary: After her mother leaves them, nine-year-old Livvy
struggles to understand and forgive as her father loses his job and
takes her and her younger brother to live in a shelter for homeless
people.
ISBN 0–689–31583–X
[1. Homeless persons—Fiction. 2. Single-parent family—Fiction.]
I. Title.
PZ7.A1824Le 1991
[Fic]—dc20   90-550
CIP
AC

T 2

For Cara, Rachel, and Stephanie

The Leaves in October

"When the leaves in October are red and gold, we'll be home," Livvy whispered in the dark.

She stared up at the ceiling from the fold-away bed she shared with her little brother, Younger, who was already asleep.

He breathed heavily next to her, with one twisted corner of an old, tattered baby blanket tucked into his mouth. Younger never let go of his blanket these days, though he was almost six.

Livvy closed her eyes tightly, but the tears rolled slowly down her cheeks and onto her pillow anyway. She wiped away the wetness with the back of her hand and felt a little bit ashamed for crying. No matter how hard she tried to hold them back, she just couldn't. She hated where she was, she hated who she was, and there was nothing she could do to change it.

She turned on her side and watched the beams of car headlights outside flicker across the walls through the high, narrow windows of the Fourth Street Shelter. Her father lay sleeping in the bed next to them. Livvy pulled her covers up to her chin and lay awake, remembering the promise her father had made.

He had promised that Livvy and her little brother would have a home again, a place of their own, where they'd be safe and happy. Livvy would have her own bed and her own room again, where she could dream her own special dreams the way other kids did. Poppy had promised them that, and Livvy had believed him. But drifting off to sleep, Livvy felt more doubtful than hopeful. Grown-ups sometimes made promises they couldn't keep, though they meant to.

Over a year earlier, in early November, the factory where Poppy worked had closed down.

At first, having Poppy at home all day was fun. He took Livvy and Younger out for cheeseburgers and ice cream, and they went to the zoo and the history museum together. The three spent more time together in those six months than they had ever before, and Younger even put his old blanket away in the back of his closet.

But when Poppy's unemployment ran out, it wasn't as much fun to have him around the trailer all the time. He began to spend more and more time sitting outside in a creaky lawn chair, staring at the squirrels and birds nesting in the trees that lined the dirt road running through the Oak Haven Mobile Home Park, where they lived.

Sometimes when she walked home from the school-bus stop, Livvy saw Poppy sitting in the chair, bent over with his face in his hands and shaking his head, or even talking to himself. She knew that something bad was going to happen.

The "something" happened when the manager of the Oak Haven Mobile Home Park knocked softly at their door one day and told Poppy that they would have to pack up their things and leave. The rent was six months late, and unpaid rent was unpaid taxes, the manager said. "Sorry," he murmured, and walked back to the office with a shrug of his bony shoulders.

Livvy and Younger helped Poppy pack whatever they could squeeze into two suitcases and some trash bags with handle-ties. The three of them stood together outside the trailer and watched the manager put a long chain and thick padlock on the door, then they took the bus into town. The Fourth Street Shelter for the Homeless was the only place Poppy could think of to go where Livvy and Younger would be safe and have a bed to sleep in.

"My children aren't going to live on the streets," Poppy whispered as they walked from the bus to the door of the Shelter together.

The people who ran the Shelter understood and took them in. They helped Poppy get the family settled, but Livvy and Younger had to share a bed because there was just one left. A lady took Livvy by the hand and introduced her to other kids about her age who lived at the Shelter too.

On the first night, Livvy was frightened. She had never had to share a place to live with so many people, and there were fifty or more people in the Shelter that night. Poppy stayed close to Livvy and Younger, and they fell asleep while he sang "Hushabye Don't You Cry," a song their mother used to sing to them. That was the night when Poppy promised Livvy they would have a home by the time the leaves in October were red and gold.

Living in the Shelter wasn't so bad in the beginning. There were other families there too. Some had just moms, or just dads, but most had children near Livvy's age. Although she was shy at first, she soon made friends. Some of the other kids had lived at the Shelter for a long time and seemed very grown-up. They showed Livvy where to do the family laundry, and where to get sheets and covers to make the beds. Livvy listened carefully, but she was too embarrassed to tell them that she'd never washed clothes in a washing machine before.

Livvy's best friend at the Shelter was a girl

named Belinda Johansen, whose family had been living there for more than a year. Mr. Johansen had worked in a factory, like Poppy. Then the owners had closed it to build a new one in another town. Belinda's father went out to look for work nearly every day, but there weren't many jobs that paid enough to get a place for all the Johansens to live. Belinda's mom was nice. She had gray blue eyes, like Livvy's mother.

The Johansens had five kids. Baby Emmett was still on a bottle. Sometimes Belinda and Livvy tried to teach Emmett shapes, letters, and colors with things they had found in the storerooms or kitchen. But Emmett wasn't ready to learn, and he tossed the "red apple for A" and "blue bowl for B" and "coffee cup for C" on the floor or up in the air. Livvy and Belinda laughed and tried again, but Emmett was stubborn.

The day Livvy and Belinda met, Belinda had asked where Livvy's mother was.

"She's not here," Livvy had told her.

"I know *that*," Belinda said. "Where is she?"

Livvy shrugged. "She's gone."

"But where did she go?" Belinda asked.

"She's just *gone*," Livvy shouted, and she walked away. She didn't want to talk about her mother, not with Belinda Johansen or anybody else. Belinda was careful not to ask about Livvy's mother again.

Livvy and Younger quickly learned all the "stay-inside" games that the kids in the Shelter played, like Chinese checkers and jacks and old maid. There were lots of toys and games, though most of them were hand-me-downs, and some were missing parts or pieces.

Since the Shelter was on a busy street, most of the kids weren't allowed to play outside, but none of them wanted to anyway. Maybe something about being homeless made kids kind of forget about the outside world. Some of the little ones had been inside for so long, everything outside frightened them.

Even after she'd been in the Shelter for weeks, though, Livvy still missed playing in the park near their trailer, and she thought of how she and Mama had taken long walks together, picking dandelions to put in the kitchen and talking to each other.

They had talked about school, about the things that were special between mothers and daughters. Mama had asked about boys, and what Livvy wanted to be. But that was before they had moved into the Shelter, before Mama had gone. Livvy didn't like to think about those days, and she struggled to push them out of her mind.

Every Sunday, Mr. Johansen and Poppy sat down and read through the job ads in the newspaper together. They smiled, nodded, or frowned at each other as they crossed off ads with their pencils, or circled them for checking out. Most jobs were for engineers and doctors, or for lawyers and accountants.

Some of the older, lonely people who stayed in the Shelter had scared Livvy and Younger at first. A few of them were sick and coughed terribly, and some smelled bad from wearing the same worn-out, ragged clothes every day.

Livvy felt sorry for them, because she knew they were all alone in the world, but what scared her was wondering if Poppy would become like them. He already had a tired, sad look in his eyes, and sometimes he forgot to shave or tuck in his shirttail.

Younger didn't get used to Shelter living as easily as Livvy or Poppy. He was only five when they arrived, and strangers still frightened him. During the first few weeks, Poppy stayed up almost every night, holding Younger and rocking him to sleep. When Livvy woke up in the morning, Poppy often would be asleep in a chair next to their bed, with his hand clutching a part of Younger's tattered blanket.

Though most of the Shelter people were nice to him, Younger cried whenever anyone he didn't know came near. No matter what Poppy said to him, or how long he cuddled him, Younger still cried. Sometimes he wet the bed, and after Poppy changed the sheets and covers, he held Younger even tighter in his arms.

Finally, Younger settled down, and he even slept through the night, though he still held on to his old blanket. He made a special friend too, an old lady whose name was Madeira. Madeira told him stories about when she had been a schoolteacher and let Younger play with whatever he pulled out of the two giant brown bags she dragged along everywhere she went. Madeira was one of the oddest people in the Shelter, and even though she was nice to Livvy, there was something a little scary about her. But Younger didn't seem to mind, and Livvy knew that Madeira's company was a lot more important than her being strange.

Most of the people living in the Shelter were very different from the ones Livvy had known at the Oak Haven. But all of them had one thing in common. They didn't have homes of their own, and that was something people outside didn't seem to understand at all.

The weeks and months passed quickly, and early summer came. October was only five months away, but Poppy still hadn't found work. He looked through the paper every Sunday, and he went out to interviews almost every day. None of the jobs paid enough to stretch for all three of them, so Poppy kept looking for something better.

Livvy noticed that Poppy was getting thinner and thinner, and that his trousers seemed to hang looser around his hips.

"Do you think he'll get like Old Pike?" she asked Belinda Johansen one day. Old Pike was one of the Shelter people who had grown so thin that his skin looked as if it were stretched across his bones. He mostly sat in a corner watching TV.

"My pa's skinny, and he's not like Old Pike," Belinda told Livvy, but her eyes looked doubtful.

Some afternoons, the two girls sat together on the front steps of the Shelter and watched passersby for awhile, trying to imagine what kind of house each one was going home to.

"That one lives in a mansion with three bathrooms, I bet," Belinda whispered to Livvy, and she pointed to a lady getting into a taxi.

"I think that man has a big apartment with a fancy whirlpool bathtub in it!" Livvy whispered as she motioned toward a man wearing a stylish suit.

Livvy and Belinda sat quietly for a few minutes, watching the people who walked by and wishing they had homes to go back to.

"I wish I could think of a way to get out of here," Livvy said quietly. "I miss going to school."

"Me too," Belinda sighed. "But we're just kids."

Livvy didn't think that being a kid mattered very much, because living in the Shelter made kids grow up faster. Shelter kids had to do grown-up things like laundry and baby-sitting, and they learned to be careful with money.

"There has to be something I can do to help Poppy get us out of here," Livvy said quietly. "I hate it here. I want my old room back!"

But Belinda Johansen shook her head.

There weren't many things Livvy could think of to do in the Shelter that she could get paid for. She and Belinda sometimes watched other people's kids when they went to job interviews, or to doctor appointments, or to the County Aid office, but nobody had money to pay them. A thank-you was usually all they got. Livvy tried to think of something to do, or something to make and sell, outside the Shelter, where people had money.

She thought about making potholders from rag strips, like the ones she'd seen selling at church bazaars, or making plant trays from throwaway plastic soup bowls. But she didn't know how to weave the rag strips to make potholders, and it didn't seem fair to use up all the finger paint in the recreation room to decorate plant trays.

Belinda told Livvy to start a wake-up service for people in the Shelter, but nearly everyone living there got up at sunrise anyway. It was hard to oversleep with forty other people moving around, washing, and making noise early in the morning. Some of the people didn't sleep at all, but only sat on their beds rocking back and forth all night. Some watched TV, or played cards, or talked to each other till sunup. There had to be something else Livvy could do.

The two girls spent hours sitting in the first-floor stairwell talking together about what they could do to help their families, but none of the ideas they had seemed right.

It was July, and Livvy still hadn't thought of anything. Poppy still hadn't found work. His promise of finding a real home for Livvy and Younger by October seemed more and more like a wish on a star or a fairy-tale ending. Livvy wanted to get out of the Shelter more than ever.

The thing about living in the Shelter that she hated most was that there wasn't any privacy at all. She didn't like how everybody watched everybody else all the time. She could hardly swallow her cereal at breakfast, because she knew people were looking at her. Sometimes Livvy felt as if she were living in a big, open cage, like an animal in the zoo.

And Livvy thought about her mother more and more often. Sometimes she saw Mama's face when she looked at herself in the mirror. She had the same round face, and the same cheekbones that slanted upward and jutted out at her temples. Livvy's hair was the same golden brown as her mother's, though her eyes were hazel with little flecks of golden color instead of gray blue like Mama's. But Livvy had the same thick, dark eyelashes, and when Livvy pictured her mother's face, Mama's eyes were always the part she remembered best. But Livvy's memories of her mother were becoming fainter and fainter.

It was hard for Livvy to accept the fact that Mama was gone. All Livvy had left of her were some clothes, a few old pictures, and a tissue rose Mama had made years ago, with a pipe-cleaner stem and edges dipped in pink food coloring. Mama said she'd made the tissue rose to wear on her high school prom dance dress, when Poppy still worked at a gas station part-time and couldn't afford a real flower corsage.

"So I made one myself," Mama had told her softly.

"Will you teach me how, Mama?" Livvy had asked.

And, one day when Poppy and Younger were outside, Mama had taught Livvy how to make a tissue rose. Livvy still remembered how to fold the tissues accordion-style and tie a rubber band tight around the middle before gently peeling apart the tissue layers to make the petals. Mama had been so proud, because Livvy made a perfect rose on her first try.

One afternoon when she and Belinda were bored, Livvy showed her how to make a tissue rose. Suddenly, Livvy realized what to do to help Poppy.

"Do you think people would buy these?" Livvy asked Belinda. They sat together in the recreation room with a large box of plain white tissues, a scissors, and a handful of rubber bands, working on tissue roses.

"If these are as nice as your mama's rose, I bet they will!" Belinda said. She was having trouble peeling apart the tissue layers of the rose she was making. She had already ruined two because the tissue ripped.

Livvy reached over and helped Belinda pull the tissue apart. "There, that's a nice one," she told her. Belinda needed more practice, though. Her roses looked all crumpled, and the petals drooped to one side. But Livvy didn't say anything. She knew Belinda wanted to help her family as much as Livvy did.

"Try another one," she told Belinda with a grin. "You're getting better."

Getting tissues to make the roses had been easier than Livvy had thought it would be. She was able to get a big box of two hundred and fifty plain white tissues from the Shelter storeroom for free, because Madeira had told the people in the office about Livvy's plan. And Nora, who helped serve meals at the Shelter, gave them a bag of rubber bands, and all she wanted was a tissue rose for herself. Livvy borrowed a scissors from the recreation room, and she and Belinda had gotten down to work.

Even Younger and Madeira helped. Younger laid the finished tissue roses in the upturned lid of a cardboard crate. Madeira punched holes in the lid edges with the scissors, then she took a long piece of heavy twine out of one of her bags and tied it through the holes. That way Livvy and Belinda each could carry a lid filled with roses by looping the twine around their shoulders.

The four of them filled two cardboard crate lids with tissue roses, but something still didn't look quite right to Livvy. The edges had to be dipped in coloring to make them as pretty as Mama's rose. But the Shelter kitchen didn't have any food coloring.

"Nobody will buy a plain white rose," Livvy moaned.

"Maybe they will," Belinda said with a shrug.

Suddenly, a shadow spread across the table where the girls sat staring at the white roses.

Old Pike coughed loudly. He looked down at

Livvy and Belinda and reached into one of his ragged pants pockets. He pulled out a plastic package of what looked like purple dust and tossed it onto the table.

"This'll work," he said in a raspy voice. "Mix it with a cup of water for color," he added. Then Old Pike walked back to his chair in the corner and sat down to watch the TV again.

Livvy and Belinda stared at the plastic package. They were afraid to touch it.

"What do you think it is?" Livvy whispered.

"I dunno," Belinda whispered back.

"Do you think we should try it?" Livvy asked, but Belinda didn't answer.

"It's print dye," a voice replied behind them.

Turning around, Livvy saw Madeira standing near the door. "Old Pike was a printer before he lost his printshop to back taxes. It'll work fine," she said.

"Get a cup of water!" Livvy told Belinda excitedly, and Belinda ran off toward the kitchen.

When she came back, Livvy opened the package, and they watched the purple dust swirl in the water and turn to coloring for the roses.

Livvy picked up the first white rose gently, and she lowered the edges slowly into the cup of purple liquid. After a few seconds, she lifted out the prettiest tissue rose she'd ever seen, even prettier than her mama's. As Livvy held the rose in her hand, she couldn't help but remember a day long ago, a day she wanted to forget.

"It's not a bad report card," Poppy said, standing in the kitchenette of the trailer. Mama sat at the tiny table, holding Livvy's first third-grade report card in her hand. She nodded slowly in agreement.

"No, it's not bad," Mama murmured. "But it could be better."

"You were the same, Olivia," Poppy said to Mama. "You never got more than C's all through school, and look how you turned out."

Livvy sat between them on one of the red vinyl kitchen chairs that surrounded the table.

"I'm sorry, Mama," Livvy apologized softly.

Her mother reached across the tabletop and

brushed a wisp of Livvy's hair back behind her ear.

"It's all right, baby," she told Livvy. "I just want you to be better than I was, that's all." She turned to look out of the window above the kitchen sink. "I want more for you than this," she whispered.

Livvy flinched as Poppy stormed out of the trailer and slammed the door.

She looked down at the tissue rose in her hand and carried it tenderly to the corner where Old Pike sat watching TV.

"It's for you," Livvy said. "Thanks."

Old Pike smiled, coughed harshly, and he lifted the small purple tissue rose from Livvy's hand.

"You'll need pins to pin 'em on," he wheezed.

But Livvy had already taken care of that.

It was hard to keep the tissue roses a secret from Poppy, but Livvy and Belinda hid them in a cupboard in the recreation room. Livvy got straight pins from Miss Albert, who worked as a part-time seamstress at a nearby dry cleaner's. Miss Albert didn't have a husband or any children of her own, though Livvy thought she'd be really good as a mom. She had nice deep brown eyes and long black hair, and she always smelled sweet even though she only had two outfits to wear. Livvy thanked her for the pins, and gave Miss Albert a purple tissue rose for free. Miss Albert pinned it to her dress right away.

When Livvy and Belinda were ready to sell the tissue roses, they decided to make a sign to put on each of the lid trays.

"What should it say?" Belinda wondered aloud.

Livvy thought hard. "How about, Please Buy a Rose?" she suggested.

"Or maybe Purple Roses for Sale," Belinda said.

"You two gotta make people *think!*" old Madeira exclaimed. "Put 'Buy a Rose for the Homeless' on those signs. You'll sell every one. People outside care, but you gotta remind 'em!" Madeira said.

Livvy and Belinda each printed out a sign on paper and taped it to the lid trays.

The signs read,

PLEASE BUY A HANDMADE ROSE TO HELP THE HOMELESS
15 CENTS EACH, TWO FOR A QUARTER

The next day when Poppy and Mr. Johansen were out interviewing for jobs, Livvy and Belinda went to the recreation room and took the lids out of the cupboards.

They helped each other loop the heavy twine around their shoulders, and they stood looking at each other nervously.

"I'm scared," Livvy confessed. "What if nobody buys them?" she worried aloud.

But Belinda looked more scared than Livvy did.

Livvy took a deep breath. "Let's go," she said, and Belinda followed her out the front door of the Fourth Street Shelter for the Homeless.

In less than two hours, every single purple tissue rose was sold.

Livvy and Belinda sat at the table in the recreation room, staring at the pile of dollar bills and silver coins in front of them. Some people had given them a dollar for a rose, though the price was fifteen cents.

One woman had pressed a five-dollar bill in Livvy's hand and didn't take a rose at all.

"I wish I had a daughter like you," the woman said to Livvy. "What's your name?" she asked.

"Olivia," Livvy gasped, holding the five-dollar bill in her hand. "But everybody calls me Livvy."

"Well, Livvy, I wish you good luck," the woman said gently, and she reached down to pat Livvy on the cheek. "You're a wonderful girl."

Livvy watched her walk down the street and then disappear around a corner two blocks away.

Belinda sold every rose in her tray too. She was only eight, a year younger than Livvy, and she'd been out of school a long time and wasn't good at counting change. But most people had helped her, or they told her to keep the change.

Neither Livvy nor Belinda could believe how nice people were to them, or how many wanted to help them by buying a rose, or two, or even three.

Later, when they counted the money, Livvy was stunned. She and Belinda had made nearly twenty-five dollars for the two trays of tissue roses.

"I can't believe it," Livvy mumbled as she touched the money.

But Belinda was laughing and dancing around the recreation room. "First, I'm going to buy a birthday present for Momma and then a new tie for Daddy to wear to his interviews!" she shouted.

Livvy looked Belinda dead in the eye.

"First, we've got to make more roses!" Livvy told her desperately.

October was only a few months away, and the leaves would begin to turn color soon.

3

_____

By mid-August, Livvy and Belinda were out of tissues and had earned nearly one hundred and fifty dollars. Livvy gave Younger and Madeira twenty dollars each for their help, though Younger gave Livvy the money back to keep for him in her Lil' Darlin' Doll Pajama Bag. Aunt Sarah had given Livvy the pajama-bag doll on her eighth birthday, which had been her first birthday without Mama. The doll had long golden hair in a curly ponytail tied with red ribbon. Gold and red were Mama's favorite colors.

Livvy wrapped a rubber band tightly around the roll of bills, and she tucked them into the doll's pajama hollow. She put the doll under the blankets of her bed and pushed it all the way to the end. The money would be safe there, and Poppy wouldn't find it by accident, since Livvy was the one who made the beds every day.

Madeira had disappeared from the Shelter with the cash Livvy gave her clenched tightly in her hand. She came back two days later dragging still another giant brown bag behind her, bulging with odds and ends. She was also wearing a strange new hairdo.

"She's got hot pink stripes in her hair!" Belinda giggled to Livvy when Madeira appeared at the Shelter door.

"Shhh!" Livvy whispered. "I can't believe it!" she confessed to Belinda. "She looks like a skunk!" Livvy gurgled, though she was quick to cover her mouth with her hand so Madeira wouldn't hear.

Long after everyone at the Shelter got used to Madeira's pink-striped hair, Madeira still stopped at the ladies' shower three or four times a day to look at it in the wall mirror. Sometimes she came out wearing little plastic flowers or tiny animal figures pinned into her pink stripes with bobby pins or silver hair clips.

For most people at the Shelter, clothing had become something they just wore without much thought. But Madeira was awfully proud of her looks and had a wild sense of fashion. She often wore very strange outfits. She could show up in a faded strapless satin gown from the local thrift shop with old construction boots on her sockless feet.

Livvy couldn't help wondering, on the days when Madeira appeared wearing something really outrageous, if she had dressed that way when she taught school. Livvy's teachers had never been so odd, but they hadn't been as much fun either. During the weeks they'd been making and selling roses together, Livvy had discovered that Madeira was a terrific storyteller, and underneath all her strangeness was a kind, sympathetic person. She didn't understand why Madeira had no one to live with or to take care of her. But Madeira didn't talk about her family, if she had one at all, and Livvy, like the other Shelter people, had learned not to ask too many questions.

Livvy and Belinda bought two more large boxes of tissues with their profits, plus a bag of pipe cleaners and a package of construction paper. Livvy planned to make tissue roses with stems for men to wear, and some with paper cutout leaves under them for ladies to wear as pins. Livvy also bought two small bottles of food coloring in the grocery store, one pink bottle and one blue, for dipping the roses in.

Keeping the business of selling roses a secret from Poppy became harder and harder. Younger nearly gave the secret away one night as the three of them sat together after supper. Poppy was counting the little bit of money he had left, with a frown on his face and a wrinkled forehead.

"Maybe you'll get a *big* surprise, Pop!" Younger squealed with a giant grin and a twirl of his old, tattered blanket.

Livvy quickly gave him a sharp poke in the ribs with her elbow, and Younger howled.

"Yeah, Poppy, maybe a really good job will come along soon and *surprise* you!" Livvy added quickly.

Luckily, Poppy was tired from job hunting that day and didn't get suspicious. But Livvy scolded her brother anyway.

"It's supposed to be a surprise!" she snapped at Younger when Poppy was gone the next afternoon.

But Younger didn't understand, and tears welled up in his eyes. Livvy felt so bad about making him cry that she apologized. She kept forgetting he was still a little kid.

"I'm sorry, don't cry. Look, just *try* to keep our secret, okay?" she told her brother softly. In a minute, Younger was grinning again. But Livvy decided to keep an eye on him when he was around Poppy, just in case he got careless again.

Nearly everyone in the Shelter, except for Poppy and Mr. Johansen, knew all about what Livvy and Belinda were trying to do. Sometimes the others helped them make tissue roses in the afternoons, when their fathers were out looking for jobs. Of course, some people were better at certain jobs than others, and some of them helped more than others did. A few of the people from the Shelter office helped Livvy and

Belinda too, but they refused to take a share of the money.

Some people thought selling tissue roses was a dumb idea and told everyone in the Shelter they thought so. But Livvy didn't pay attention to them. Madeira explained that it wasn't easy for them to watch Livvy and Belinda making money when jobs for grown-ups were so hard to find and most of the people living in the Shelter had lost everything they had. They'd lost their jobs and their homes, and some had even lost their families.

"Jealousy's an easy thing to feel when you've nothing to call your own, and the little bit you have is from charity," Madeira said apologetically.

But Livvy already understood.

She felt jealous too sometimes, and angry very often. Everything around her—every toy, every book, and even every stitch of clothing she wore—was used. She didn't have a single thing that was new. Even her favorite sweater, in yellow wool with white scallops around the collar, had belonged to someone else first. So Livvy knew why some of the Shelter people didn't have the heart to wish her well. Madeira, Old Pike, and Miss Albert were enough, and they made up for the others who couldn't stifle their jealousy. At least some wanted to do something to help Livvy and Belinda.

Old Pike tried to make tissue roses at first, but he had arthritis in his hands, and he couldn't fold the tissues right. But he was great at dipping. The tissue roses he dipped always came out beautifully, with perfectly colored edges. Livvy and Belinda let him do all of the dipping.

Madeira was good at folding the tissues, so Livvy had her fold and tie them with rubber bands. Then Livvy and Belinda gently pulled the tissue layers apart to make the rose petals, and they passed the roses to Old Pike for dipping. Together, the four of them could finish four or five trays of tissue roses in only one afternoon.

Younger was absolutely the best at selling roses. In a few hours, he could sell more tissue roses than Livvy and Belinda combined.

"He's got a face like an angel. *That's* what sells," Madeira confided. "Younger reminds them that 'homeless' means little kids, and not just old fools like me," she explained. "They could use more reminding, too."

Livvy had to admit that Younger was handsome. He had Mama's big, dark-lashed, gray blue eyes, and he had Poppy's thick, black, shiny hair. And Younger *did* sell more roses than anyone else, so Livvy trusted Madeira's judgment. Every day Younger went outside with a tray of roses, and within a few hours he came back inside for another tray. Old Pike said he was a natural.

Younger would be six years old August 26. Livvy could still remember the day Mama came home from the hospital holding her new baby brother in the blue blanket he still slept with. His thin little fingers had fluttered like a butterfly's wings, and Livvy saw tiny blue veins beneath the skin on his hands.

"Isn't he beautiful?" Mama had whispered to Livvy, who was then almost four years old. Livvy had peeked over the blanket at the new baby. He was small and wrinkled, and his cheeks were bright pink and waxy.

"He's *ugly*!" Livvy had cried, and she backed away. But Mama chuckled, and she kissed the baby's fingers gently. She motioned for Livvy to come close to her, as if she had a secret to tell, and Livvy came nearer.

"He'll get nicer as you get older, Livvy," Mama murmured softly, putting an arm around her and lightly kissing the top of her head. Livvy looked down into the baby's gray blue eyes.

"What's his name?" she asked.

"Francis Hopkins Junior," Mama said. "But Poppy wants to call him Younger, since he's the younger Francis now." Mama had sighed a long, peaceful sigh.

"I'll tell you something, Liv. Nothing will ever be as important as your family. I promise that's true," Mama whispered, cuddling her new son with one arm and hugging her small daughter with the other.

But as Livvy watched Younger fill up another tray with finished pink tissue roses to sell outside the Shelter, she reminded herself that promises were one thing that grown-ups didn't always take as seriously as kids.

Poppy had promised to have a home of their own by the time the leaves in October were red and gold, but it was already August, and Poppy hadn't even found a job. The more Livvy thought about it, the more she realized that Poppy could have made the promise for a special reason, maybe because *he* needed to believe it more than she did. Poppy sometimes cried at night too. Livvy had played opossum, and she had seen him try to muffle his sobs with his pillow.

Shelter life was probably much worse for him than for Livvy and Younger, because grown-ups were ashamed when things went wrong, even if it wasn't their fault. Livvy didn't blame Poppy, but she knew that he blamed himself. The promise of a home by October might have been a way for Poppy to keep hoping and not give up.

But Livvy wished that Poppy hadn't made the promise. If he couldn't keep it, if there wasn't a home when the leaves in October were red and gold, Livvy would never be able to believe him again, just as she had stopped believing Mama. Then there wouldn't be anyone for Livvy to believe in but herself, and she dreaded feeling that kind of loneliness.

By late August, the tissue-rose business had made more money than anyone expected. Livvy counted over one hundred dollars in just her share, less Younger's share of the money. Her plan was to give Poppy the surprise after Younger's birthday on August 26. She was considering Labor Day, in the first week of September, as a good day for the surprise. It was a holiday, and Poppy wouldn't be out on interviews that day.

She tried to decide what to give Younger for his birthday, but that wasn't easy. There were lots of toys to play with at the Shelter, and Younger was the kind of kid who liked to play whatever someone else was playing. He wasn't the type who wanted to do anything by himself.

Livvy thought about getting him a game he could play with the other kids, or maybe some clothes from the thrift shop. But Younger already had a game he liked best, Chutes and

Ladders, and he didn't care about clothes the same way Livvy did.

"Why don't you get him something for school?" Belinda suggested one afternoon after Livvy mentioned her brother's birthday.

"We don't *go* to school, remember?" Livvy replied. School was a sore spot to Livvy, because it was one of the things she missed the most. In third grade, Mama had begun helping her with reading and math, and Livvy's grades had improved to B's and even some A's. Just when Livvy was beginning to like school and do well, everything went to pieces. Regular school was just a memory now.

Although Shelter kids were supposed to go to a local school, many of them didn't. Schools needed the records from the last schools kids had gone to, and sometimes the records didn't arrive in time to get them into the right classes, usually at odd times in the school year. So Shelter kids sometimes got put back in lower grades, where the other kids often teased them. Going to school could be worse than not going at all.

Older kids took the bus or walked, but little

ones had to be taken. If parents were out looking for work, it was easier to leave their kids at the Shelter.

"Not going is the best reason of all to get him something for school!" Madeira laughed. "Tell you what. If you get him some easy books, I'll help him a bit," she volunteered.

For a moment, Livvy thought that Madeira was making one of those grown-up promises that she was reluctant to count on. But Livvy didn't want to give up on grown-ups altogether.

"If I get him a few books at the thrift store, will you teach him to read?" she asked Madeira, who nodded.

"Could you teach Emmett too?" Belinda begged.

"And . . . maybe . . . us?" Livvy added, glancing over at Belinda, who looked at her in astonishment.

Madeira let out a low chuckle.

"Well, it's been a long, long time, but I guess I can still teach you rascals," she replied grudgingly. "You have to promise me to work hard and not waste my time!" Madeira warned, wagging a bony finger at them.

"It's a promise!" Livvy answered, grinning.

Finally, after so many months of feeling helpless, Livvy had a chance to change something for the better. She would buy Younger books for his birthday, and then Madeira could teach him to read. That would be Poppy's first surprise.

Livvy would give him the *real* surprise on Labor Day. She could hardly wait to see his face when she handed him the money she had made from selling tissue roses outside the Shelter. Everything was going be okay, she thought.

After all, Livvy had never made a promise *she* couldn't keep.

4

Livvy heard a soft voice whisper near her ear, "Time to get up, honey."

But the covers felt so good around her, and the early-morning light was dim and comforting. She opened her eyes just a little, and she scanned the room. The ball fringe at the bottom of her blue curtains bobbled and bounced in the breeze blowing gently from the window screen. Beside the window, a stack of clean, folded clothes lay on top of her blue wooden chest of drawers. She had forgotten to put her clothes away again. Livvy threw back her covers and sat up in bed. She'd better put the clothes away before Mama noticed them, or she wouldn't be allowed to go to the carnival in the park over the weekend. She didn't want to miss the carnival. Livvy always won a stuffed animal or two to bring home.

"Liv, get up!"

"I *am!*" she called, and she swung her bare feet off the bed and onto the floor.

But the floor her feet touched was the dingy, gray vinyl floor of the Fourth Street Shelter. She'd been dreaming again. Livvy sat on the foldaway and hugged her pillow to her chest. The dreams about Mama and her old room in the trailer were always so real.

Quietly, without waking up Younger, Livvy got up and walked down the hallway from the sleeping rooms toward the ladies' shower to wash her face and brush her teeth. Looking in the wall mirror, Livvy knew she'd have to get going if she wanted to go to the thrift shop and be back before lunchtime, when Poppy would return to the Shelter.

Belinda came along too. She brought some of her money and rolled it up with Livvy's to stash in Livvy's right sneaker. The two girls went out the front door of the Shelter and turned right.

The thrift shop was two blocks away and already crowded when they walked in.

Livvy found several books to choose from for Younger that were back in a corner of the shop among dozens of old used books stacked nearly to the roof.

"This one's good. It's *Little Toot,* the one with 'I think I can, I think I can'," Livvy said to Belinda, who was leafing through some of the musty grown-up books. She had found one with pictures of people who were nearly naked, and she didn't even hear what Livvy was saying.

"Eeech, look at this!" Belinda squealed, and she held up the book and showed Livvy a picture. "Gross," she whispered and wrinkled up her nose.

Livvy reached over and flipped the book cover to look at the title.

"It's *Anatomy.* It's how doctors learn stuff about people's bodies," she told Belinda.

"It's a school book?" Belinda asked in amazement. "I'll never study ana'my—it's disgusting!"

"It's an-at-o-me, and I don't think there's much chance of you having to learn it soon,

Bee," Livvy said with a laugh. "C'mon, let's pay for these."

The two girls wiggled their way through the aisles crammed with old clothes and shoes and furniture toward the pay counter. Livvy pulled the roll of dollars out of her right sneaker and gave the lady behind the cash register four dollars for three books for Younger and a pale pink fuzzy winter scarf for herself.

"Why are you buying a scarf? We hardly ever go outside," Belinda asked.

"It's pretty and I like it, that's why," Livvy responded. "And I'll *be* going outside soon."

She wrapped the scarf around her neck, although that day was one of the hottest of the summer. Along with her new scarf, Livvy wore a smile all the way back to the Shelter. Younger's birthday was the next day, and she was going to the day-old bakery to get a birthday cake for him. So far, everything was going according to her plan.

Madeira was pleased with the books Livvy bought for Younger.

"*Little Toot* is a perfect start," she told Livvy.

"But what about you and Belinda? Didn't you promise me you'd take lessons too?" Madeira questioned.

"There are books in the recreation room we can use," Livvy answered. She was able to read very well, nearly two grades higher than her fifth-grade level. "I'll pick some out for Bee too," she assured Madeira, "and we'll be ready whenever you say."

Madeira seemed satisfied with that answer. "The day after Younger's birthday, we'll get started," she instructed. "I'm going to enjoy this, I think!" With a crack of the knuckles on her left hand, Madeira waddled off toward the ladies' shower. That morning, she'd pinned a Chinese paper fan into the hot pink stripes of her hair, and it wobbled as she walked away.

"Do you want to go to the day-old bakery with me?" Livvy asked Belinda.

"I can't," Belinda said with a shake of her head. "I have to help Momma with laundry today."

"Will you keep an eye on Younger while I go?" Livvy asked. "Just for a while?"

"Sure," Belinda said.

Livvy checked the amount of money she had tucked in her sneaker. There was enough to buy a sheet cake that was big enough for everyone in the Shelter to have a piece. It wouldn't be as nice as the cakes Mama used to make, but it would still be better than no cake at all.

Livvy's seventh birthday had been the last one when Mama made a cake. By then, the factory where Poppy worked had cut back hours, and Poppy was only working two and a half days a week. Their money was running out quickly, but Mama had managed to buy enough woolen yarn to knit Livvy a pink scarf. Livvy's birthday was the week before Christmas, and she needed a warm scarf to wrap around her neck when she walked to the school-bus stop.

"It matches your pink-and-white coat," Mama had said proudly when Livvy opened the wrapping paper with the scarf inside. "I hope you like it, Liv," she had added worriedly.

Livvy loved the scarf. She wore it all through the winter, but it was stolen, or perhaps taken by mistake, at school the next March. Now, almost three years later, Livvy missed that scarf more than any of the things the family had to leave behind in the trailer when they moved into the Shelter. The pink scarf was the last thing Mama had given her.

Livvy's mother loved birthday parties, and she had always decorated the inside of the trailer for them with whatever was handy. On Younger's fourth birthday, Mama had borrowed a set of Tinkertoys from a neighbor. She'd put together over a dozen little Ferris-wheel shapes and tied them to string, which she ran across the window rods inside the trailer. When she tugged the string, all the Ferris wheels started to move and jump at the same time. Younger had loved that, and he spent most of the time at his birthday party tugging the string to set the wheels jumping and turning above his head. Mama had always found ways to get around their tight budget and have a good time on very little money.

On her way to the day-old bakery, Livvy was determined to do the same, and make Younger's sixth birthday party fun for him, even if he had to spend it inside a shelter for homeless people.

The cake Livvy picked out was enormous, and it had green flowers and little golf clubs on it. But Happy Birthday was written in green icing on the top, so it would be just right. The lady at the bakery counter told Livvy it was made for someone who played golf, but it hadn't been picked up. So it was for sale as a day-old.

"It's for my brother," Livvy told her. "He's six tomorrow."

The cake cost five dollars. The bakery lady put it inside a big white box and tied it up with string so Livvy could carry it. Livvy had already bought a small box of colored birthday candles to put on the cake. With the long box in her arms, she very slowly walked back to the Shelter, and then into the kitchen, where she slid the box on a shelf inside the giant silver refrigerator. Nora agreed to guard it until it was time for Younger's party.

That night, Livvy was so excited she wasn't able to fall asleep easily. Everything was ready, but she kept going over details in her mind. Younger's cake was safe in the kitchen, his books were wrapped in some shelf paper that Madeira had given her, and the rest of the money from selling tissue roses was under the covers. Livvy could feel the pajama-bag doll at the end of the bed with her toes. Poppy would be so surprised. Livvy only hoped the money was enough for Poppy to use as a rent deposit on their new home, the one she yearned for, the one with a yard covered by the leaves in October. Finally, Livvy fell asleep.

Livvy woke up and got Younger washed and dressed to have breakfast in the dining hall. Breakfast was always the worst time of the day for Livvy. She was often sleepy and uncomfortable standing in line with the homeless mothers and children who waited for juice, toast, and bowls of cold cereal. The grown-up men hardly ever ate breakfast with them, though they would stop in the dining hall for a hot cup of coffee before going out to look for work. Poppy did that every weekday. He'd get a cup of hot coffee without powdered cream, see to it that Livvy and Younger each got some breakfast, and he would go out to look for work, still rubbing the morning sleepiness from his tired eyes. Poppy arrived in the dining hall only a few minutes after Livvy had taken Younger through the breakfast line.

"Morning, sweetie. Sleep okay?" he asked Livvy in a hoarse voice. He was always a little raspy throated before he had his coffee.

"Yeah, okay, Pop," Livvy answered. "You have an interview today?" she asked.

Poppy nodded. "Yep," he replied. "I've got a good feeling about this one too."

Livvy leaned close to her father and whispered, "Don't forget Younger's party at lunch."

Poppy winked at her slyly, gave her a kiss on the cheek, and stood up from the table.

"Got to get going. Wish me luck," he said. "I'll be back for lunch, Liv," he added with a smile.

"Good luck, Pop!" Younger gurgled around his mouthful of cornflakes.

"Good luck, Poppy," Livvy said softly.

She turned to her brother. "Speed it up, huh? I've got to wash some clothes before lunchtime, and I want you to take a shower and put on clean stuff today," she told Younger firmly.

Livvy had been doing part of the laundry for

the last six months, but she didn't mind. Washing clothes was just another of the things that Shelter kids learned to do before most other kids. Livvy felt fortunate that there were only three of them, and they wore clothes for a week before doing wash. The laundry room was always crowded with kids doing laundry, some for families much larger than her own.

Younger wrinkled his nose at her. He hated taking showers in the Shelter. Livvy couldn't take him into the men's shower room by herself, so she had to drag him, usually whining, into the ladies' shower instead. Younger was afraid the girls would see him without clothes on, though Livvy always stood watch at the door to the shower stall while Younger soaped up and rinsed off. She had learned to get Younger into the shower room early, because the hot water usually ran out by ten in the morning, and there was nothing worse than hearing him holler while taking a shower under cold water.

Livvy put a load of clothes in one of the three old washing machines in the Shelter laundry room. She had bought a small box of detergent at the office for a quarter, and she poured it in the machine. With a twist of the dial, the machine began to swish.

Younger took his shower obediently, and Livvy got him dressed in clean blue jeans and a T-shirt. He hadn't even the slightest notion that it was his sixth birthday. But that would make the surprise party even better, Livvy decided. After Younger was clean and dressed, Livvy sent him off to the recreation room, where some other kids close to his age were playing Twister.

Nora was in the kitchen helping prepare the lunch meal.

"Is the cake okay?" Livvy asked, watching Nora make peanut-butter sandwiches.

"Fine," Nora answered.

But Livvy went to check the refrigerator anyway. Younger's green-and-white cake still lay undisturbed on the shelf where Livvy had placed it.

"I'll be back at twelve-fifteen," she told Nora, and returned to their sleeping room to make the beds. After that, she would put the washed clothes in one of the giant dryers in the laundry room. By then, Poppy would probably be back.

A few minutes after noon, Poppy strolled in the front door of the Shelter with a huge grin on his face. Livvy sat in the recreation room, watching Younger trying to stretch his legs from a red dot on the Twister game to a yellow dot.

"Are we ready?" Poppy whispered to Livvy, leaning down over the back of the old sofa where she sat.

Livvy lifted her eyes to look at her father. "You bet. He's going to be really surprised, Pop!" she whispered back.

"He's not the only one," her father replied mysteriously. "I'm ready when you are, Liv."

Livvy nodded, got up, and went into the kitchen. Nora helped her stick the candles into the cake and light them. Holding Younger's cake in her arms, Livvy made her way slowly through the kitchen doors to the recreation room. When she began to sing "Happy Birthday," everyone in the room joined in the song.

Younger was so surprised, he looked around at the others, wondering whose birthday it was. But when Livvy stopped in front of him, with the candle flames flickering, Younger realized it was *his* birthday.

"Make a really good wish," Livvy told him.

Her brother closed his eyes tightly. When he opened them, he blew out every candle on the cake.

"Hope we both get our wishes," Livvy told him softly, and she kissed her little brother's cheek.

5

Younger had a wonderful birthday party. Just about everyone he liked, and who liked him, was there. Old Pike and Madeira helped him open his presents, including one from each of them. Old Pike gave him a set of block alphabet letters from his old printshop. Madeira gave him a Sesame Street puzzle. Poppy gave him a Whiffleball-and-bat set. By the time he got to the present from Livvy, his cheeks were bright red with excitement, and his eyes sparkled.

He ripped the wrapping paper to shreds, and he looked down at the books in his hands. He tried to smile, but the uncertain look in his eyes was too hard to hide.

"Will you read them to me, Livvy?" he asked shyly. "I can't by myself."

"That's another present, Younger," Livvy told him with a giant smile. "Madeira's going to have school for all of us. Right here in the Shelter. You're going to learn to read!"

Poppy looked at Livvy warmly, and tears appeared in the inside corners of his eyes. Younger stood up holding *Little Toot* in his hands.

"I'm going to read, Poppy—all by myself!" Younger nearly screamed.

"That's great, son," Poppy said as he turned to Livvy. "You're a very special girl, Liv. Very special," Poppy said softly, and he hugged his daughter tightly. "I love you very much," he murmured, folding his arms around Livvy.

Livvy felt a peacefulness that was a new feeling to her, a warmness that spread through her, head to toe, like a gentle breeze. In her heart, she knew that it was probably similar to what Mama had felt every time she had done something to make Livvy or Younger happy. And Livvy liked the feeling very much.

After Younger opened his presents, after everyone had at least one piece of birthday cake, after Younger ran off to play Whiffleball with the other kids in the basement hallway, Poppy took Livvy by the hand and sat down with her in the recreation room.

"I've got another present, and it's for both you and your brother," Poppy said seriously.

Livvy's heart thumped in her chest. She wondered if wishes made on birthday candles could come true so fast. She made herself take a deep breath.

"What, Poppy?" she managed to ask, though her throat felt tight and knotted.

Poppy lowered his head and studied the palms of his hands for a moment. "I got a job today, Liv," he said softly.

"Oh, Pop!" Livvy shrieked. "We're leaving!" Livvy jumped up and was about to run to the basement to tell Younger the news when Poppy reached out and grabbed her arm, pulling her back.

"Liv, it's a job working on the interstate highway, doing repairs," Poppy murmured.

"That's okay, Pop," Livvy told him, but she was puzzled by the strange look on her father's face. He didn't look as happy as he should have.

"I've got to leave here, and the two of you can't go with me," her father blurted out. "I've got to put you in a foster home for a while."

Livvy felt the blood inside her rush down through her neck and arms, and she felt sick to her stomach. She bent down, putting her head on her knees.

When Livvy's dizziness passed, Belinda was peering at her so closely their noses almost touched.

"Livvy?" Belinda asked worriedly.

"Where's Poppy?" Livvy questioned sluggishly.

"I'm right here, baby," her father's voice assured her, and Livvy felt his hand stroke her hair. He was kneeling over the end of the sofa behind her head.

Livvy struggled to sit up. Heavily, she managed to lift herself. Her stomach was still churning.

"Liv?" she heard her father say softly, and

finally she turned to look at him. His eyes were red from crying, and there were dark circles under them.

"It doesn't matter, Pop," Livvy mumbled. "But you better tell Younger." She stood up slowly and walked away, toward the ladies' shower room, leaving her father behind. He watched her disappear down the hallway and behind the gray steel door.

Livvy ran the cold water fast and hard, scooping up handfuls and splashing her face in an attempt to stop the tears that poured from her eyes and down her cheeks and the sides of her nose. But it was no use. She turned off the faucet, leaned against the faded tile of the washroom wall, and slid down to the floor, where she crumpled into a heap and cried as she had never cried before, not even when Mama had left.

Livvy had known something was terribly wrong between Mama and Poppy. She had sensed that something, unspoken and sad, flowed between them from the time she was able to understand the words they spoke to each other. It wasn't so much *what* they said to each other as it was the *sound* behind the words. There was a sharp, angry edge to their conversations that even Livvy felt at only six. The sharpness made her uneasy, but at the time she didn't know why.

Often one of them got mad at the other and slammed a door or threw something at a wall inside the trailer, though it was never anything big or anything that would break into dangerous pieces. Mostly, Mama threw clothes or pillows, and Poppy threw shoes or paperback books. Then one or the other would storm off to be alone for a while. Later, neither one would mention the fight between them. Mama would pick up the clothes or pillows she had sent flying, or Poppy would scoop up his shoes or pages of the books from the floor, and then there was silence. But the quietness was even worse than the noise of slamming or throwing.

Then, suddenly, one day Mama was gone. Most of her clothes were still hanging in the metal wardrobe in the bedroom, so none of them realized at first that she wasn't coming back. Her brush and comb and hand mirror were gone from the dresser top, and some of her makeup was gone from the bathroom shelf, but no one noticed these things right away.

Later, when Mama still hadn't come home, Poppy began to look around the trailer and realized that some of her things were missing. Mama hadn't taken much with her, so Poppy told Livvy and little Younger, who was only three and a half then, that Mama probably had gone to stay with her sister, their aunt Sarah, in Virginia for a few days. But Livvy heard Poppy talking to Aunt Sarah later that night, and Aunt Sarah told him that Mama wasn't there.

The next day, Poppy called the police to report Mama missing, but the police told him he would have to wait until more than two days had passed without any word from Mama for her to be labeled as a missing person. That night, Poppy didn't sleep very much. Livvy heard him moving around in the kitchen almost all night. She knew something had happened, but she wasn't quite sure what it was.

The day after that, Poppy got a letter in the

mail from Mama, but he never told Livvy what it said.

"Mama isn't coming back," he had said to Livvy, and he went outside to work on the pickup truck. That was all Poppy said, and that was the last thing he ever said about Mama leaving. Livvy didn't understand why Mama left, or where she had gone, and Poppy wouldn't talk about it. But he was right, because Mama had not come back. She hadn't even said good-bye.

Sitting on the floor of the ladies' shower room, exhausted from crying, Livvy wished she were dead. She brushed back her hair with her hands, clenching the locks above her temples in her fists. She wiped her nose with the back of her shirt sleeve, drew a deep breath, and stood up.

She told herself that she should have known. Grown-ups made promises as easily as they breathed in and out. But they did not keep them. Livvy would never believe another grown-up promise.

She threw back the door to the shower room

and walked briskly into the recreation room. Poppy and Younger sat huddled together on the sofa, and Younger was crying. She came up behind Younger and laid her hand on his shoulder, looking at her father directly.

"It's all right, Younger. We'll be okay," Livvy said, but the words came out sharply and unevenly.

Poppy gazed up at her behind the sofa with the eyes of a man who had lost everything. "I'm sorry," he whispered hoarsely. "I swear I'll be back for you."

But Livvy looked away. She was finished with promises now. She walked around the edge of the sofa, took her brother's hand, and pulled him up. Younger followed her meekly toward the kitchen. Livvy took out a gallon jug of apple juice and poured a small amount into a paper cup. She watched as Younger tried to swallow the juice.

"I'll stay with you," she murmured to her little brother, and she stroked his shiny black hair. "I won't ever leave, Younger. Not ever." Her heart felt as if it were breaking apart inside her chest as she watched her little brother fight back the tears he wanted so badly to cry.

The two sat quietly on stools beside the long silver metal table in the kitchen. They were on their own now, Livvy decided, but they had the money from selling tissue roses, which was nearly two hundred dollars. Two hundred dollars would be more than enough money. Two hundred dollars would take them both as far away as they wanted, or as far away as they could get, from a foster home.

The bus station was only four blocks west of the Shelter. There was no reason for Livvy to give Poppy the money now. He was leaving them, as Mama had done years before, and he didn't deserve it. Livvy drank a glass of apple juice and tried to decide where she and her brother would go.

"Would you like to see the ocean?" she quietly asked her brother.

Younger stared at her wide eyed and nodded his head. Without telling him what she was planning, Livvy would buy two tickets on the next bus going to Norfolk, Virginia. That was where Mama had been born, where she grew up, and the place she left when Poppy got a job at the factory in Pennsylvania.

And Livvy was going there. Maybe she and Younger could stay with their aunt Sarah. Maybe, just maybe, that's where Mama was.

Poppy walked into the kitchen, and Livvy took her brother by the hand. They walked out to the recreation room with their father trailing behind them. Livvy leaned down near Younger's hair.

"Go wash up for supper," she told him softly, and she gave him a gentle push.

When Younger reached the door of the men's shower room, he turned to look at Livvy and Poppy. With a wave of her hand, Livvy told him to go in. Younger obeyed.

"Livvy, we've got to talk about this," Poppy said calmly. "I can't leave without knowing you understand."

Livvy ignored him.

"I've got to wash up," she mumbled, and she

walked away from her father. When she reached the door of the ladies' shower room, Livvy did not turn around to look at her father as her brother had done.

6

Later that night, Poppy told Livvy about his new job working on the highway, and about the foster home he'd arranged for Livvy and Younger to stay in while he was on the road. Younger was in bed, and Livvy and her father sat together in the recreation room.

"It won't be so bad, Liv," he said earnestly. "It'll just be for a few months, and these people are really nice. They've got a big house, and a big yard. You won't hate it. You'll get to go to school like other kids."

"We want to stay with you," Livvy argued. "Why can't you take us?"

Poppy's shoulders slumped. "I'll have to stay with the other men, Liv, in dirty roadside motels. It's not good for kids to live like that," he answered.

"How much worse than this could it be?" Livvy angrily demanded, and she flung her arms out and pointed to the Shelter walls. "We belong with you."

"Livvy, I just can't," Poppy whispered. "God forgive me, I *can't* take you two along. I'll come back for you as soon as I'm able."

Livvy turned away from him furiously. But then she turned back.

"You're a liar, and I hate you!" She spat the words at her father. "You're just like Mama."

"Oh, Liv, no . . ." Poppy moaned, and he reached out to touch her shoulder, but Livvy pulled away from his hand.

"Don't come back," Livvy insisted. "If you leave without us, we don't want you anymore, or your promises either."

Livvy buried her face in her arms and cried while her father sat helplessly beside her in the recreation room. She didn't care how bad he felt. He was leaving them behind, and he'd broken his promise.

🐦　🐦　🐦

Livvy left the recreation room and went to bed. She didn't bother washing or brushing her teeth, but only crawled beneath the covers beside her brother and lay awake looking up at the lights dancing beyond the high windows of the room. Younger's even breathing was comforting. She pulled the covers up a little and tucked the edges in near his shoulders. At least she had Younger. The two of them would always be together.

But as far as Livvy was concerned, Poppy was already gone. It was time for Livvy to make the plans now, even if she was afraid. Grown-ups just couldn't be counted on. Livvy felt a strange sense of freedom in finally accepting that fact, and though she wasn't even ten yet, she felt older and stronger. She and Younger would be all right. Livvy would make sure of that. But they weren't going to any foster home, or any place where they weren't wanted and they didn't belong. They would be all right, but only as long as they took care of themselves, and never believed in another grown-up. But as Livvy fell asleep, her strength and the sense of freedom she'd felt at first gave way

to an awful, aching, terrible pang of loneliness.

"Up and at 'em!" someone barked above her.

Livvy opened her eyes. Madeira, wearing an
ugly orange dress with giant yellow flowers
printed on it, looked down at her. There was a
tiny paper umbrella stuck in her hair. Livvy
turned over and glanced at the bed next to
theirs. Poppy was already up and gone. She
looked back at Madeira, who stood above her
with her hands firmly on her hips.

"Get your breakfast, girl, and then it's time
for class," she said. "A half an hour in the rec
room. Him too." She pointed at Younger, who
still slept. Madeira turned on her shoeless feet
and left the sleeping room.

Livvy shook Younger's shoulders.

"Rise 'n' shine," she whispered.

Younger's eyes opened slowly. "Hi, Liv," he
said sleepily. "I'm six."

Livvy grinned. "That's right, kiddo. You're
six."

"I'm going to read all by myself," he said
softly.

"Madeira's waiting to teach you after break-fast, so get going," Livvy told him.

Younger sat up, stretched his thin arms, and got up to walk to the men's shower room. His black hair stuck up a bit in the back. Livvy reached out to smooth it.

"Don't forget your toothbrush," Livvy said, and Younger grinned sheepishly. He picked up his toothbrush and the tube of toothpaste from their night table and walked out of the room. He obviously didn't remember what Poppy had said the day before about leaving.

Livvy lay back in bed for a few moments before she got up. She would have to make Younger understand that Poppy was leaving them, and she didn't look forward to doing that. When Mama had left, he had been too little to really feel a loss. Little kids could get used to whatever happened, and whatever changes came along. But Younger wasn't a baby any-more, and when Poppy left, he would be fright-ened and hurt.

Livvy reached down under the covers and touched the pajama-bag doll. She felt the big roll of dollars, squeezed it, and withdrew her arm from under the spread. Then she got up from the bed and got ready for breakfast. When she returned from the washroom, Younger was waiting for her, holding his *Little Toot* book on his lap. The two went down the hallway and the stairs into the dining hall.

After a breakfast of French toast, juice, and milk, Livvy looked across the dining hall to where Belinda sat with her family. She motioned to Belinda to meet her in the recreation room. Livvy took a paper napkin, got it wet with a little water, and tried to wipe the maple syrup from Younger's fingers. She didn't want him to ruin his book with sticky hands. Then Livvy and Younger went to the recreation room to begin their lessons with Madeira.

When they reached the recreation room, Livvy nearly froze at the door. Madeira had changed outfits since early that morning. Now she wore a plain shirtdress and black flats on her feet, and her hair was pulled back into a kind of ponytail. She even had on glasses.

"What's wrong with her?" Younger asked his sister. "She's different."

When Livvy caught her breath, she smiled at Younger. "She looks like a real teacher, doesn't she?" she said, giggling.

"Holy ham hocks!" someone gasped behind Livvy and Younger. It was Belinda, and she was as surprised by Madeira's new appearance as they were.

All three children walked into the recreation room cautiously. Madeira pointed to several chairs near a small card table in one corner, and Livvy, Belinda, and Younger sat down without a word.

"I've got some paper and pencils for you," Madeira began, "and I've chosen a few books for you girls to start with."

She placed a copy of Louisa May Alcott's *Little Women* in front of Livvy, and a worn copy of E. B. White's *Charlotte's Web* in front of Belinda.

"I understand you have a book of your very own to use," Madeira said to Younger with a smile.

Younger grinned as widely as he could and

held up *Little Toot*. Madeira nodded. "Good choice," she said approvingly.

Madeira got Younger started on writing the alphabet, and she helped Belinda read the first chapter of *Charlotte's Web*. Livvy opened the copy of *Little Women* and began to read to herself silently, but she kept drifting off in plans and daydreams. Her mind just wasn't on reading.

After almost two hours, Madeira let them rest and get ready for lunch.

"After lunch, we'll do a bit of math work," she instructed.

"What's math work?" Younger asked excitedly. He was enjoying "school" very much.

"Numbers," Livvy answered. "You learn to add numbers together, like what's one plus one."

"Four!" Younger shrieked, and Livvy and Belinda howled with laughter.

"Two plus two is four," Madeira said patiently, and she shot a sour look at the girls. "We'll start slow, Younger, and you'll see how easy math is. Now go get ready for lunch."

Younger and Belinda got up, stretched, and

waited for Livvy. But Madeira told them to go on to the dining hall because she wanted to talk to Livvy about something. Younger wasn't eager to go anywhere without his sister, but Belinda took his hand, and he followed her trustingly.

"I'll come in a few minutes, Younger," Livvy called after him. She sat stiffly, thinking she was going to get a lecture from Madeira on not concentrating on her book reading.

But Madeira sat down next to her, sighed, and said, "I'm sorry about the foster home. I've had three kids who were raised in foster homes, and every one is smart as a whip and happy too," she confessed to Livvy quietly.

"You have kids?" Livvy asked in astonishment. She wished she could control the surprise in her voice, but she wasn't able to. The idea of Madeira being a mother was too big a shock.

"They're all grown now, but they were three of the most beautiful babies you've ever seen," Madeira replied in a whisper. "I know how hard it is for your dad to do what he's got to do, honey, but believe me, it's a darn good thing he's doing."

"Good for him, maybe. Now he doesn't have to worry about us. He can just go wherever he wants," Livvy answered solemnly.

Madeira was visibly concerned. "Honey, there isn't going to be a single day till he comes back for you when he won't worry," she insisted. "You have to trust me on that."

Livvy looked at her and laughed. "I'll never trust another grown-up as long as I live!" she snapped.

Madeira nodded. "I understand that you've been disappointed . . ." she murmured.

"Disappointed? Lied to is more like it!" Livvy argued. Her voice cracked with the strain of holding back tears that were choking her throat.

"No," Madeira said calmly and firmly. "Your pop didn't lie to you. He just couldn't make it all work out the way he promised it would. That's different."

"Sounds like a lie to me," Livvy mumbled.

Madeira leaned in nearer to Livvy. "Whoever told you that grown-ups can do anything they want any more than kids can?" she asked softly. "Don't work that way at all, honey. They get cut short more than anyone."

Livvy sat silently for a moment. She really hadn't ever thought about Poppy not having *his* part of the promise come true.

"Just think it over," Madeira said gently, "and try to understand what your pop is feeling." She lightly touched Livvy's hand before getting up and walking to the recreation room door toward the dining hall. But at the door, she stopped and turned back toward Livvy.

"I never went back for my babies. Your pop's not going to make that same mistake, Liv," she said. "He's got more courage and love in him than I ever had in my whole life." Then she turned back and left the room.

Livvy sat alone in the recreation room, staring glumly at the floor. She didn't want to think about what Poppy was feeling. She felt too much hurt of her own. But Madeira's words echoed in her mind as Livvy rose and walked slowly to the dining hall, where her brother waited.

As she walked, Livvy thought of all the terrible things she had felt long ago, when she had finally understood that her mother was never coming back. It was the first time Livvy had really considered how awful Mama's desertion must have been for her father, and, as she entered the dining hall, she knew deep in her heart that Poppy had suffered enough. There wasn't any good reason for Livvy to hurt him any more.

After lunch, Livvy took Younger back into the recreation room to wait for Madeira. But Younger was feeling a bit restless, and he wouldn't sit still. He kept running off in all directions, though Livvy did her best to catch him and keep him there. Finally, Madeira showed up. There were yellow mustard stains down the front of her shirtwaist dress. The Shelter had served hot dogs and beans for lunch, and Madeira liked a lot of mustard on her hot dogs.

Old Pike strolled in behind Madeira, holding a small chalkboard in his arms. He put it down on top of the card table and walked off to the corner where the TV was. His favorite soap opera was on at one o'clock every weekday, so he made sure to be in the recreation room early so he'd have control of the TV channels. Sometimes, there would be arguments between the people who wanted to watch different shows, but no one ever argued with Old Pike. They watched whatever he watched until he was finished watching.

"Now let's get to work," Madeira said. She handed Livvy and Belinda each a piece of paper with addition and subtraction problems printed on it. "You have a problem, you ask me," Madeira said.

She pulled Younger closer to the card table on his chair and picked up a tiny wedge of white chalk. "You and I are going to learn about numbers, sweetie," she said.

But after a few minutes of working on the math problems, Poppy walked into the recreation room with a strange woman. The two of them stopped where Livvy sat bent over the work sheet Madeira had given to her.

"Liv, this is Mrs. Burwinkle from Social Aid," Poppy said to Livvy softly. "I'd like you to talk with her for a minute or two."

Mrs. Burwinkle was sharply dressed in a slim gray tailored suit, and she smiled broadly at Livvy from where she stood.

"What about?" Livvy asked suspiciously.

Poppy glanced at the strange woman helplessly.

"About the things that are bothering you, Olivia," the woman answered gently. "I want to help you get used to the idea beforehand."

Livvy looked at the woman calmly.

"You got any kids?" Livvy questioned.

The woman nodded. "Yes, two," she answered.

Livvy frowned. "You don't know anything about what's bothering *me*," she stated. "Your kids still got a mom," Livvy snarled, surprised by the anger in her own voice.

The woman moved a little closer to Livvy, and she leaned down a bit.

"Love doesn't disappear that easily, Olivia, and neither does anger," she whispered gently. "There's always love, together or apart, and anger too."

Livvy hid her face in her hands for a moment.

"You better talk to us both, then," she said weakly, motioning toward Younger.

"I'd like to do that," the woman replied. "May I interrupt your class for a while?" she asked Madeira, who nodded slowly at her.

Livvy took Younger's hand, and the two followed Mrs. Burwinkle to a quiet corner of the recreation room.

7

Mrs. Burwinkle stayed about a half hour, sitting in the corner with Livvy and Younger and talking softly about the foster home Poppy had arranged for them to stay in while he was on the road. She was very sympathetic, and Livvy got the feeling that she really cared about them. But it wasn't enough to soothe all the hurt Livvy was feeling.

Younger got very upset when he finally understood that Poppy was really going away without the two of them. Though Mrs. Burwinkle tried to convince him that going to a foster home didn't mean he wouldn't see his father ever again, Younger couldn't get that into his head. What he understood was that Poppy was leaving, the way his mother had done. He didn't remember much about Mama, but he had learned that "gone" meant gone forever.

Mrs. Burwinkle struggled to calm him down. She was quite pretty, and her deep green eyes had a soft glow about them that gave her face a tender look.

"The family you'll stay with is named Calloway. They haven't any children of their own, and they'd like to help you while your father is away," Mrs. Burwinkle explained slowly to Livvy and Younger. "They understand that your father will come back for you, and they want him to come back."

Livvy felt as cold as stone. "Why can't we go with our father?" she demanded.

"Didn't he explain that he must live on the road with the crew?" Mrs. Burwinkle asked gently.

"We could stay together someplace else," Livvy argued. "If he wanted us with him."

Mrs. Burwinkle sat back and straightened her shoulders. "Olivia, if he took you with him, he would have to spend all the money he'll be paid on motel rooms and food," she said softly. "He wants to save his earnings so that when he comes back, the three of you can have a home together."

"He won't come back," Livvy said solemnly. "He'll never come back for us."

Mrs. Burwinkle leaned toward her. "Trust him, Olivia. He loves you and your brother very much," she murmured.

Livvy considered saying something nasty to Mrs. Burwinkle about trusting grown-ups, but she decided to keep quiet because Mrs. Burwinkle might suspect that Livvy had something planned other than going meekly to a foster home.

"Will you let me take you to meet the Calloways the day after tomorrow?" Mrs. Burwinkle asked. "Just meet them, and then we can talk some more."

Livvy looked at her brother. His eyes were wide with fear. She reached out and took Younger's hand.

"I think we should meet them, Younger. To see what they're like before we decide," Livvy stated. She knew Younger would go along with whatever she said or did.

"Good," Mrs. Burwinkle said, pleased. "Your father will be relieved, and you'll make the Calloways very happy."

Mrs. Burwinkle spoke to Poppy quietly for a few minutes, shook his hand warmly, and left the Shelter. Afterward, Livvy sat in the recreation room, and she considered what Mrs. Burwinkle had said about the Calloways.

But Livvy didn't think it should be up to her and Younger to "make the Calloways very happy," and it certainly wasn't fair. Livvy thought it was time, finally, to make herself and her brother "happy." Whether or not the Calloways were pleased, or her father felt relieved, was of no importance to Livvy.

She was bone weary of doing things to make someone else happy, and she was angry. She was angry about selling tissue roses so that Poppy would have enough money for a rent deposit on a place for the three of them to live, when all Poppy was planning to do was leave them behind. She was angry at Poppy, and still angry at Mama for leaving them long ago. Most of all, she was angry at herself for believing that October would be special and set apart from the other months. Because October was going to be just another month. Livvy no longer cared about October's red and gold leaves. All she cared about was getting away from all of the adults who had lied to her.

To make things worse, Belinda Johansen's father got a job too, the kind of job that let him stay in one place and keep his family with him. The Johansens were moving out of the Fourth Street Shelter the first week of September, into a three-bedroom apartment. So Belinda was walking on air and talking nonstop about the new apartment, where she would share a room with her little sister, Angelina, and Livvy hated that.

It wasn't really Belinda she hated, of course, though Livvy just couldn't seem to stand being around her anymore. What she hated was Belinda's good luck. What she wanted was to be Belinda instead of Livvy, and what she needed was to feel that somebody, somewhere, was going to take care of her instead of running away. That was the worst feeling of all, much worse than being angry. It was the feeling that made Livvy snap at Belinda and hurt her feelings for no reason. Livvy felt out of control. She just couldn't stop mean things from coming out of her mouth. Belinda spent less and less time around her.

Poppy tried to be extra nice to Livvy and Younger after Mrs. Burwinkle left. He did laundry and made the beds. He even took the two of them to the zoo, the way he used to before they moved to the Shelter. He had a job now, so there was no reason for him to be gone all day long. But spending time with Poppy wasn't the same as it had been back then, when Livvy had known the three of them were still together as a family.

It was different now, because Poppy was constantly saying he was sorry for leaving. Neither Livvy nor Younger really had a good time with him, because they were too busy thinking about how Poppy was leaving soon. Poppy seemed to be distracted and worried too. The three of them walked around the zoo like robots, not really able to enjoy seeing the animals or being outside.

Two nights before Livvy and Younger were supposed to go with Mrs. Burwinkle to meet the Calloways, Poppy put Younger to bed a little early and sang "Hushabye" to him. Then he took a small blue envelope from the bottom of his suitcase, from inside a tiny zippered compartment, and he gave it to Livvy when the two of them were sitting in the recreation room.

"What is it?" Livvy asked in a dull voice. She didn't really care what it was.

Poppy rubbed his knees with the palms of his hands. "It's a letter from your mother, Liv. She sent it to me a long time ago, and she told me to give it to you when I thought you were ready to read it," he said awkwardly. "I think you should read it now."

Livvy held the blue envelope in her hands as if it were made of ice crystals and would break apart with the slightest touch. It was a letter from Mama, for her and no one else. She was excited, and at the same time terrified to open the envelope and read the letter.

Mama had been gone more than a month when Livvy began to have nightmares that sent her screaming out of her bed and into the trailer kitchen. She dreamed, over and over, that she and Mama were climbing trees together in the park across from the Oak Haven Mobile Home Park. In the dream, Livvy would watch as Mama climbed the biggest tree in the park. The tree was so tall that the top of it couldn't even be seen from the ground, and had clouds swirling around the upper branches. But Mama would climb the tree easily, laughing as she swung from one giant branch to the next. About halfway up, Mama would stop and look down at her, motioning for Livvy to follow. Livvy would begin to climb, struggling to hold onto the huge boughs of the tree.

"I want more for you than this," Mama would call down to her as Livvy climbed up and up. Then, when Livvy was just a few inches from her, Mama would reach out her hand to

Livvy. Mama looked like an angel, balanced in the fork of two branches of the tree, gazing down at her young daughter as if from heaven. Livvy would climb and climb, and finally her hand would clasp her mother's. Expecting Mama to pull her up from where she sat so gracefully, Livvy would stand up on the branch.

But instead of pulling her up, Mama would let go of Livvy's hand, and Livvy would see herself falling helplessly to the ground.

She always woke up at that point in the dream, soaking wet from sweat and screaming, "Mama!" Poppy would rush from his bedroom, banging into the sides of the trailer walls in a half sleep. He would catch Livvy, out of bed and running blindly, in his arms. The dreams lasted for almost a year after Mama left.

Now, Livvy sat with a letter from her mother in her hands, unsure of what to do. Her first instinct was to read it, devour it, memorize every word of it. Her second instinct was to tear it up, unread, and throw it in the trash bin. Her curiosity, and her love for her mother, won out over her resentment, and Livvy carefully pried open the flap of the blue envelope. She had to know what Mama had said to her, and she hoped to learn and understand why Mama had gone away and never come back.

My darling Olivia,

I've asked your father to give you this letter at whatever time he thinks you are ready to read it. He doesn't know what it says, and he has promised to give it to you unopened.

By now, I've been gone for a long time, and you must hate me for leaving you and your brother as I did. That is understandable, but I hope that you won't hate me forever for what I've done. I will try to explain it to you and then ask you to forgive me for not being a better mother to you and Younger.

When your father and I got married, we were very young, just out of high school, and we thought that we were very much in love with each other. We moved to Pennsylvania when your father got a job at the factory there. You already know this part, because I've told you about it.

The part that you don't know is that I was still just a young girl then, and so afraid to leave Virginia and my own family. I wasn't grown-up at all. I even slept with an old stuffed teddy that my daddy gave me when I was very little.

And then you were born, and I didn't know what to do. I was the youngest in my family and had never taken care of anybody before. Sarah always took care of me, and Alfred was even older than Sarah. So I cried a lot, because I was scared that I would do something wrong and hurt you by mistake. Your dad didn't know how to help me take care of you, being from a family of all boys, and you being a beautiful china-doll-pretty little baby girl. So I tried to take care of you by myself, on those long, lonely days when Poppy worked double shifts at the factory. I sang songs to you while I held you in my lap outside the trailer. Do you remember the "Hushabye" song I liked to sing to you? Maybe not, as it was long ago.

Then Younger was born, and I tried to take

care of him too. I don't think I did a very good job, because Younger was sick a lot when he was a baby. Luckily, he seemed to get stronger every year. But I was getting sicker all the time, Olivia, from being alone most of the time, and poor, and afraid, and only twenty-one with two babies already. It was never that I didn't love you and Younger, because I did, and still do, so very much.

But I wasn't old enough to take the strain when Poppy lost his full-time hours and the money ran out. There was hardly enough money to pay rent and feed you babies. I got to feeling that we were all going to starve to death, and your father and I began to fight with each other, for no reason but that we were both so scared. We said terrible things to each other, most of which we didn't really mean, but that just came out because we were still so young and without experience.

I tried, and Poppy tried, but our marriage wasn't a very good one. I believe that if we had waited awhile longer to get married, maybe until we both had good jobs, we might have been able to make our marriage work out real well. But we didn't wait, and we had you babies so soon, and we were too young and without enough education.

Somewhere along the line, I got to thinking that maybe I should give up and go back to my family in Virginia. Basically, I was just being a little girl instead of a grown-up, and what I wanted to do was run away like a child. You probably thought about running away before, maybe even when you heard me and your father yelling at each other or throwing things. I understand, because I felt the same things, Olivia. But let me tell you right now that running away is not the best thing to do when something hurts you. Because when you run away, you don't change anything. You just leave it the way it is, and you worry about it and feel bad about it, all the days of your life.

That is how I feel about you and Younger. I will worry and feel bad all the days of my life that I left you behind with Poppy. I left because I was scared and young and still a little girl. Someday, I hope that I will be grown-up enough to come back to see you, and it is because of that hope that I'm asking you to forgive me, and to explain to Younger that I didn't leave because I didn't love him or you. I loved you more than anything, and I still do.

I left because I was weak and afraid, and I wasn't a happy person with your father. It is not his fault either. It is nobody's fault. It is just bad luck and bad planning, because if I had been older and smarter, I think your poppy and I could have been happy to-gether.

That is what I wanted to tell you, and that I love you now and always. Please don't hate me, Olivia. I hope so much that we can all be together someday when I am sure that I can take care of you the way you need to be taken care of. Forgive me because I ran away. I was selfish and scared. But I am trying ev-ery day to be a better person, and maybe I will be good enough someday to deserve you.

I love you, my most beautiful and wonderful daughter.

Mama

8

Livvy sat in the recreation room with Mama's letter in her hand for a very long time, not really thinking as much as feeling what Mama had written to her. Poppy had gone to play rummy with some of the men at the Shelter in one of the sleeping rooms, so aside from Old Pike, who watched the TV in the corner as he always did, and a few other people scattered about the room, Livvy was alone with her feelings.

After a while, she got up from the sofa and walked to their sleeping room. Livvy threw back the covers, reached down under the sheet, and took out the pajama-bag doll. She unzipped the compartment where she had tucked the big roll of dollars, took out the money, and threw the empty doll onto the bed. Then she walked down the hallway looking for her father.

She found him with a group of four other men in Mr. Dantelli's sleeping room, and she walked up behind him.

"Hi, Poppy," she said.

Her father smiled and turned, slipping one of his arms around her and pulling her up to the table.

"Hi, Liv. What do you think?" Poppy asked her softly, showing Livvy the cards he held in his hand.

"I think this is for you," Livvy answered, and she tossed the roll of bills onto the table in front of her father.

"Where did this money come from, Livvy?" her father asked a few minutes later. He'd gotten up from the card table right away, snatched the roll of bills up in his hand, and ushered Livvy out of the room. They stood in the hallway together.

"I made it," Livvy answered truthfully.

"How? This is a lot of money, Liv! There has to be a hundred dollars here," he gasped.

"One hundred ninety-six dollars," Livvy stated matter-of-factly.

"Livvy, where did this money come from?" her father asked urgently.

Livvy looked up at her father's pale, thin face. "Younger and Belinda and I made tissue roses and sold them outside the Shelter when you were out looking for work," she said. "Madeira and Old Pike and Miss Albert helped us, and some of the other people from the Shelter helped too."

"I don't understand," her father muttered.

"I taught everyone to make tissue roses like Mama used to make, and we sold them for fifteen cents each," Livvy explained. "That's how much we made."

Her father's whole face seemed to collapse in on itself, and his cheekbones seemed to sag around the lines near his mouth. Livvy could almost feel his heart breaking inside his chest, just by the look in his eyes.

"Oh, Livvy," he managed to say hoarsely.

"It's for you to use on the road so you don't have to spend what they pay you," Livvy stated.

"I can't take this money, Liv, it's yours and Younger's," Poppy whispered. "You earned it by yourselves." He looked down at the roll of dollar bills in his hand.

"It's *our* money, Pop," Livvy insisted. "We're a family, and we've got to help each other out."

Her father reached out and grabbed her, pulling her toward him forcefully and burying his face in her hair.

"You kids are more important to me than anything," he said in a cracked voice.

Livvy knew that Mama had been right about running away. It wouldn't change anything. It was better just to stick it out and try to change things as much as she could, even if it meant that she and Younger would spend the special month of October in the home of the Calloways, far away from their father and the home they so desperately wished for. The letter from Mama had made it all clear to Livvy, even though she still ached to have Mama's arms around her again. Livvy finally understood. And she finally forgave.

🍂　🍂　🍂

Two days later, Mrs. Burwinkle showed up just after breakfast to take Livvy and Younger to the Calloways' for a visit. Livvy had put on her best dress and had cleaned Younger up and put a small tie around the neck of his only white shirt. Poppy was wearing the only sport coat he owned, and he looked very nervous.

"This is going to be fun, and the Calloways will adore you both," Mrs. Burwinkle told the children confidently. "And your father will know that you're both safe until he can come back for you," she said.

The three of them drove out to the Calloways' house in Mrs. Burwinkle's little red car. Livvy tried to figure out where they were going, but it had been a very long time since she'd seen any part of the city but the few blocks surrounding the Shelter, so she lost track of where they were. In about fifteen minutes, the four of them sat in the red car together in front of a beautiful light blue house with a pretty redwood fence around it. A dog with floppy ears sat near the fence looking out to the car, its tail wagging quickly left and right.

"They've got a dog, Livvy!" Younger squealed, and he leaned out of the back window. "Hiya, pup!" he called to the dog, which barked happily at him and wagged its tail even faster.

"Looks nice, Liv," Poppy said softly. "Don't you think so?"

Livvy nodded but didn't say anything. No matter how nice the house was, or how nice the Calloways were, it still wasn't going to be easy, and they still weren't her family.

"Well, then, let's go visit," Mrs. Burwinkle said happily, and she opened her door.

The four of them got out of the car and walked up to the redwood fence together. Younger walked a bit faster, because he wanted to pet the dog.

Livvy felt a little bit awkward at first, but it was worse for Poppy, who couldn't seem to sit still at all during the visit. His hands shook, his knees bobbed, and his eyes darted all over the rooms of the Calloway house.

Mrs. Calloway was older than Mama had been, and older than Mrs. Burwinkle, but she had the most astonishing red hair Livvy had ever seen. She wore it swept up on the sides and set with a silver clasp on top of her head, the back all in curls falling to her shoulders. She had blue eyes, but they were light blue and not gray blue like Mama's or Younger's eyes. She was very nice too.

Mr. Calloway was thin and full of energy, and he kept pulling Poppy this way and that way through the house to show how he'd "expanded" the rooms of the house to make it more "spacious." Mr. Calloway was evidently a good carpenter, because Poppy seemed to admire the work he had done very much. Mr. Calloway was dark haired, though not as dark as Poppy, and he had small wisps of silvery hair streaked through the curls near his ears. Both Mr. Calloway and Mrs. Calloway were very friendly to Poppy, and extra-special nice to Livvy and Younger.

"This will be Livvy's room, if it's okay with you," Mr. Calloway said to Poppy, and he leaned in to flick on the light switch. The colors pink and white appeared everywhere, on the wallpaper and furniture and bed and curtains. There was even a small hope chest at the foot of the bed that had been stenciled in pink and white flower buds.

"It's beautiful," Poppy replied sincerely. "Isn't it beautiful, Liv?" he asked, looking down at his daughter, who gazed in at the room that would be hers.

"Uh-huh," Livvy managed to say. She had never seen such a beautiful room in her whole life.

"And this is Younger's room," Mrs. Calloway piped from across the hallway.

Livvy and her father moved toward the room, almost afraid to look at it. Inside, the furniture was all gleaming polished wood, and the bed was a bunk bed, the kind that boys always liked so much. A giant toy chest in the corner was open, and it was filled with all kinds of new, shiny toys. Younger was drawn inside like a honeybee to a rose. He knelt beside the toy chest and just stared into it, trying to identify all the different things inside.

The whole group eventually went back into

the comfortable living room, where Livvy and Younger were allowed to watch TV while the grown-ups talked to one another in quiet voices.

The Calloways were nice, the house was perfect, and though Livvy knew she should be feeling happy, there was still a stab of pain shooting through her ribs as she sat on the floor with her brother. But Younger looked as if he were in heaven, watching Nickelodeon on the cable TV and sitting beside the floppy-eared dog, stroking its ears happily. The dog's name was Kermit, like the frog on "Sesame Street," and it took to Younger right away.

After about two hours, Mrs. Burwinkle told them it was time to go back to the Shelter, and Livvy and Younger followed her and Poppy out to the car. The Calloways stood at the redwood fence and waved good-bye, and Livvy could tell they were wishing with their whole hearts that it would work out.

"They don't have any kids of their own," Livvy said aloud in the car.

"No, they don't," Mrs. Burwinkle answered

from the driver's seat as she steered the car back to the Shelter.

"Why not?" Livvy asked.

Poppy nudged her. "That's kind of private, Liv," he cautioned.

"No, it's all right," Mrs. Burwinkle insisted. "Mrs. Calloway had some female troubles, and although she is well now, she can't have any babies," Mrs. Burwinkle answered honestly.

"You mean like a hysterectomy?" Livvy questioned.

Mrs. Burwinkle seemed shocked for a few seconds that Livvy would know about such things, but Livvy read a lot of the women's magazines that were donated to the Shelter. She had read about all of this in *Cosmopolitan* and *Woman's Day*.

"Well, yes," Mrs. Burwinkle said, recovering from her surprise. "A hysterectomy."

"Why don't they adopt a kid?" Livvy inquired.

"They're trying to, Olivia, but the waiting list is very long, and they're a little bit older than usual to adopt a little baby. That's why they want to be foster parents," Mrs. Burwinkle said carefully.

"Oh," Livvy replied. "That's good," she added when she'd thought about it for a few seconds. "They're very nice people."

"Yes, they are. I'm glad you like them as much as I do," Mrs. Burwinkle responded.

"I like Kermit best," Younger chimed in, and Poppy squeezed him tightly.

"I like *you* best." Then Poppy chuckled, but it was Livvy's hand he held all the way back to the Shelter.

The next day was Labor Day, a holiday for everyone. It was a kind of joke around the Shelter, because most of the people didn't have any "labor" to take a holiday from. Mostly, everyone sat around the recreation room that day, playing cards, watching TV, and talking.

Poppy hadn't mentioned the foster home since they had come back to the Shelter from the Calloways'. He'd been very quiet since then, which kind of worried Livvy. When Younger was playing Chutes and Ladders with his friend

Matthew Jones, Poppy sat down beside Livvy on a gray plastic chair in the recreation room. She looked up at him, saw that he wanted to talk, and she marked her place in *Little Women* and closed the book.

"What is it, Pop?" Livvy questioned.

"Did you like it?" he asked her. "The Calloways' house, I mean. And the Calloways."

Livvy nodded. "They were real nice, Pop, and the house is neat. We'll be fine," she told her father, hoping that she sounded convincing enough.

"Good," he muttered. "Good. I like them too."

"It'll be okay, Pop. Younger and I will be fine till you come back," Livvy told him urgently. She didn't want him to feel worse. She knew now how hard it was for him to leave them behind until he could take care of them, the way Mama had wanted to do but couldn't. At least Poppy had been brave enough and strong enough to stay with them until now.

"It'll be okay," Poppy echoed, but his voice was empty and light, as if it had had all the feeling sucked out of it. "I'm going to play some cards and think," he said, patting Livvy on the arm. Poppy stood up and walked over to the rectangular table where Old Pike was dealing pinochle hands. Livvy found her marked place in *Little Women* and went on reading.

The next day, Poppy woke up and left early, but he left a note to Livvy stuck to his pillow with a safety pin.

"Back around suppertime. Love you lots," the note said, and Livvy figured that Poppy just had some things to do, or maybe wanted to go to the Social Aid Office by himself to make the final arrangements with Mrs. Burwinkle for when he would take Livvy and Younger to the Calloways'.

She woke her brother up, got him showered and dressed, and the two of them went down to the dining hall for breakfast. After having a little of the hot oatmeal cereal and bacon strips that Nora and the others were serving for breakfast, Livvy and her brother headed toward the recreation room together. Younger's friend

Matthew was playing hopscotch on a grid he'd chalked onto the hallway floor, and Younger stayed there to play along, so Livvy went to the recreation room alone.

Belinda Johansen was waiting for her inside. She sat with her tiny white Miss Piggy suitcase on her lap, dressed in a pretty yellow dress.

"Hi, Livvy," she said softly. "We're leaving today, and I wanted to say bye to you."

Livvy no longer felt angry with Belinda. Instead, she felt a kind of happiness for her.

"I'm sorry I've been mean to you lately," Livvy managed to say in apology. "I was kind of jealous is all."

Belinda grinned. "You don't hate me?" she asked in wonder.

"No!" Livvy laughed. "I don't hate you at all," she said to comfort her friend.

"Will you come spend the night sometime?" Belinda asked. "Angelina can sleep in with Josh and Adam, and we can stay in my room."

"I'd like that a whole lot, Bee," Livvy told her friend. "But I won't be here."

"Where're you going?" Belinda asked.

"To a foster home," Livvy told her. "But they're real nice people, and Poppy is coming back for us in a little while."

"Gosh!" Belinda exclaimed.

"Tell you what," Livvy said. "Write down your address on this paper, and I'll let you know where I am. Maybe I'll call you up on the phone."

"Okay!" Belinda said excitedly, and she carefully printed the address of the apartment where she and her family were moving.

"Maybe I'll see ya soon," Livvy said happily, and she gave Belinda a hug. Then Belinda's mother beckoned from the doorway, waved warmly to Livvy, and led Belinda out of the Fourth Street Shelter for the Homeless forever.

9

Poppy didn't get back to the Shelter until well after suppertime. At first, Livvy had worried that he'd run off or something, because of how bad he felt about having to put Livvy and Younger in a foster home. But he did come back, though he looked really tired. Younger was sitting in Madeira's lap in the recreation room while she read him a story. Livvy sat leafing through a *People* magazine.

"Sorry I'm late," Poppy said, putting his hands on Livvy's shoulders.

"Poppy!" Younger called, and hopped off Madeira's lap to run to him. Poppy caught him and swung him up onto his shoulders.

"Did you have some supper?" Livvy asked her father with concern.

"You're always worrying about me, aren't you?" Poppy teased her. He slid Younger off of his shoulders and set him down on the recreation room floor. "I think it's about time I let you off the hook," Poppy added mysteriously.

"I'm not on a hook, Pop," Livvy told him, but she wasn't sure what he meant. He looked as though he had become ten years younger in only a few hours. His dark eyes sparkled, and his smile just wouldn't stop stretching from ear to ear.

"Yes, you are, and you're off," her father insisted. "Everything's taken care of now."

Livvy put down the *People* magazine with a firm slap.

"What are you talking about, Pop?" she asked.

But her father just grabbed her by the hand and pulled her toward the front door of the Shelter, laughing all the way. Younger followed behind them with Madeira, the two of them skipping and prancing toward the door.

Livvy walked out of the Shelter behind her

father and stopped on the concrete stairway. Poppy stood under the streetlights with his arms thrown wide toward the street.

"Well?" he asked excitedly.

"Well, what?" Livvy asked in confusion.

"Do you think it's big enough for all three of us?" her father asked very cautiously, and he leaned back against a small, faded green camper-trailer parked at the meter in front of the Shelter.

"The owners took three hundred forty for it, and that's with the kitchen pots and pans and bed linens," Poppy said slowly. "That leaves me fifty or so dollars for travel, plus what I'll make on the road while I'm working. It's old and not in great shape, but it'll do."

Livvy's mouth opened like a parachute. She wanted to say something, to scream, to laugh, anything. But nothing came out. Nothing at all.

Poppy walked toward her, and he knelt down in front of her on the sidewalk. Several people outside stopped to stare at him, but Poppy didn't seem to care.

"I'm taking you two with me, Livvy. I'm not going to leave you, not ever," he whispered.

"What?" Livvy finally was able to exclaim, as she scanned the outside of the camper. "What about the Calloways, and your paycheck, and being on the road?" she was able to force out.

Poppy stood up, walked toward Younger, and picked him up. He looked at Livvy warmly.

"I called the Calloways this morning and told them. They're good people, Liv, and were really happy for us. Mrs. Burwinkle feels the same way," he said. "Besides, we're a family, and we've got to help each other out," he declared. "Someone very smart told me that," he added with a wink. "Someone I can't live without."

Livvy screamed and ran into his arms, nearly knocking Younger onto the ground. The three of them stood squeezing each other, while Madeira and Old Pike, who had followed them outside, danced a jig around them happily.

A few weeks later, the Hopkins family sat around a small campfire somewhere in Missouri, roasting hot dogs on sticks for supper. Younger chattered about the kids he'd met that day in the campsite two rows down, and Livvy kept scolding him for burning his hot dog in the fire. Every now and then Younger would let his stick drop right into the flames. He had a lot to learn about campfires and how to be careful around them.

Poppy laughed and bit into his hot dog eagerly as the mustard he had spread on it squished out through the sides of the bun. Roadwork made him really hungry. A drop of mustard landed on his work shirt.

"Here, Pop," Livvy said, and she tucked a paper napkin over the first button on his shirt.

"Thanks, my beautiful, wonderful daughter," Poppy said softly. Livvy and Poppy had grown much closer over the last month, and Livvy had let him read the letter that Mama had written to her. He'd kept quiet after reading the letter, but some of the hurt seemed to have gone from his eyes afterward.

They watched the fire glow and snap and crackle near the lamplit inside of their camper, and when the night grew too cool to stay outside, the three of them went in to bed. Livvy went to sleep in the fold-down bed she still shared with her little brother.

The camper was small and cramped, and the water tap didn't always work. The camper certainly wasn't what Livvy had expected when she had wished for a home where the three of them could be together, but other wishes had come true.

At night, through the worn screens of the camper windows, Livvy could smell the autumn leaves that gently fell to the ground from the trees shading the campsite. After all that time living in the Shelter, Livvy was just beginning to realize what really being "homeless" meant. Surrounded by October's blanket of red and gold, she thought of Madeira, Old Pike, Nora, and Miss Albert, and she knew that she had something that they probably would never have.

Though Livvy didn't have the house she'd dreamed of, she had Poppy and Younger, and even Mama, whose thoughts Livvy knew were with her. Soon Poppy would have enough money saved for an apartment deposit, and Livvy and Younger would be able to go to school again and be like other kids. Poppy had promised, and Livvy knew now that her father kept his promises, even if it took a bit longer to keep them than he planned.

But "when" didn't matter so much to Livvy anymore. Now, the most important thing to her was that the three of them were together. As long as they were together, Livvy knew, no matter where she was, she was "home".